Romance Once Again

N.S. Nandvanshi

Published by N.S. Nandvanshi, 2024.

This is a work of fiction. Similarities to real people, places, or events are entirely coincidental.

ROMANCE ONCE AGAIN

First edition. December 27, 2024.

Copyright © 2024 N.S. Nandvanshi.

ISBN: 979-8231157945

Written by N.S. Nandvanshi.

Table of Contents

This book is all about an second chance in a Relationship which led to an call back of both soals

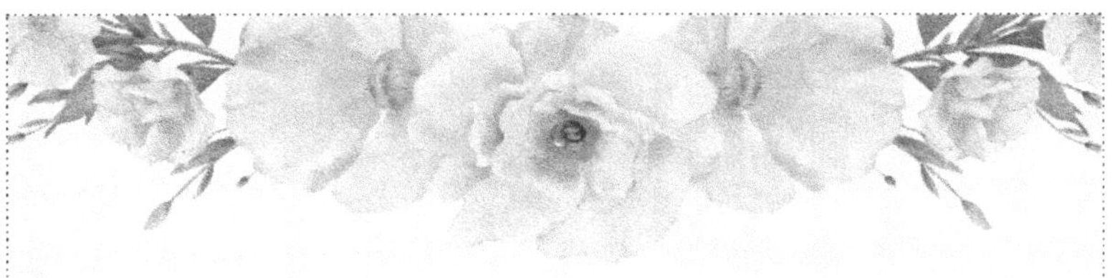

N.S NANDVANSHI

ROMANCE ONCE AGAIN

A Romantic IRONY

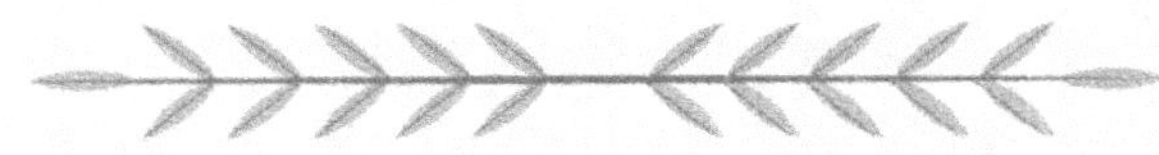

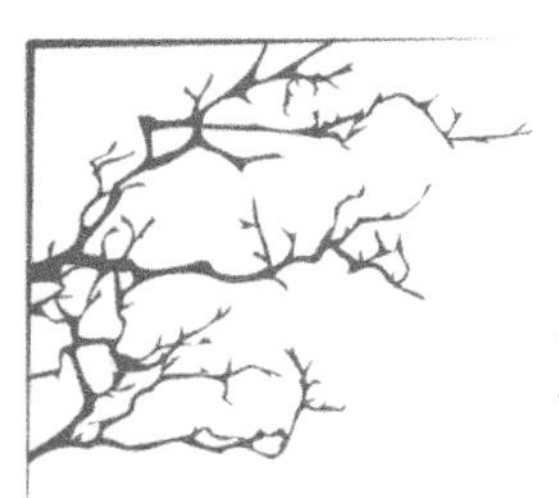

Dedication

To everyone who believes in second chances, in love, and in the beauty of rediscovering oneself.

<u>Acknowledgments</u>

This book would not have been possible without the endless support of my family and friends, who never stopped encouraging me to write from the heart. To the readers who embark on this journey, thank you for trusting me with your time and emotions. And to love—in all its forms and complexities—for being the muse of this story.

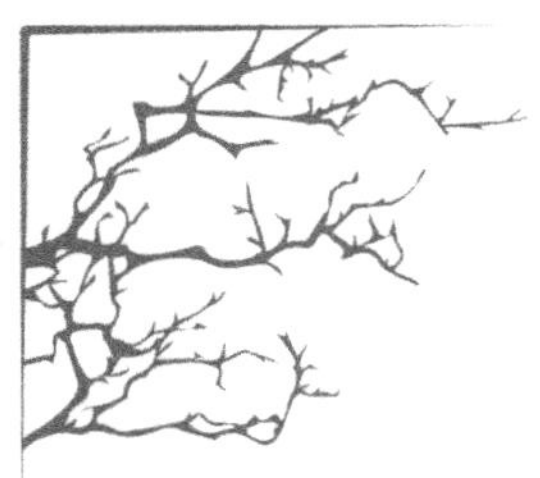

Prologue

Love is not always a linear path. It weaves, it turns, it breaks, and it rebuilds. Sometimes, it's not about finding the perfect person but about rediscovering the magic within yourself. This is a story of such a journey—of love lost, love found, and the courage to embrace it once more.

Table of Contents

Chapter 1: The Unlikely Reunion

I t was a bright, crisp morning in the city of Delford, where the hustle of daily life was always in full swing. The streets buzzed with people, their faces a mixture of purpose and indifference, as they moved swiftly toward their destinations. Amid the crowds, Lily Williams walked at a slower pace, her eyes gazing absently at the passing buildings. There was something different about today. Something that felt like a quiet storm on the horizon.

Lily had been back in Delford for just two weeks. The city she had once called home felt strange now, foreign even, after so many years of living away. The people had changed. The places had changed. But Lily had changed the most.

She had come back to settle her late mother's affairs, but there was something else that called her here. An unresolved chapter in her life, one that still haunted her every time she thought about it. He.

As she walked past the small café on the corner of Maple and 5th Street, a bell above the door jingled. She paused and glanced inside. The café hadn't changed. It still had that familiar warm glow, the same barista behind the counter, and the same jazz music softly playing in the background. But what caught her attention was a figure sitting by the window—a man with dark, tousled hair and an almost haunting smile.

Her heart skipped a beat. It couldn't be.

Lily stepped back, her breath catching in her throat. Her eyes widened as the realization hit her. It was him. Ethan Carter. The boy she had once loved with all her heart. The boy who had broken it just as easily.

She took a deep breath, her mind racing. She hadn't seen Ethan in over five years, not since that fateful day when their lives had veered in completely different directions. Yet, here he was, sitting just a few feet away, like no time had passed at all.

Ethan glanced up, his eyes meeting hers. For a moment, neither of them moved, as if the world had stopped, just for them. Then, slowly, a smile tugged at his lips, as though he had been waiting for this moment just as much as she had.

Lily's heart fluttered in her chest. She had come back to Delford to move on, to find peace. But seeing him again brought back all the emotions she had buried for so long.

"Hey, Lil," Ethan said, his voice the same, as though no time had passed. He gestured to the empty chair across from him. "Care to join me?"

Lily hesitated. The familiar warmth of his presence was both comforting and terrifying. She was no longer the young girl who had once been so in love with him, but the feelings were still there, lingering beneath the surface. With a deep breath, she walked toward the table and sat down.

"You've been back for a while now, haven't you?" Ethan said, his eyes searching hers as though trying to read her thoughts.

"Two weeks," Lily replied, her voice steady despite the whirlwind inside her. "Settling my mom's affairs."

"Ah," he said softly, nodding as if understanding. "I'm sorry about your mom, Lily."

"Thanks," she said, offering him a faint smile. "It's been... hard. But I'm managing."

The conversation felt like it was starting again, as if no time had passed at all, and yet everything had changed. Lily couldn't decide if it was comforting or unsettling.

"Are you planning to stay for long?" Ethan asked, his gaze softening.

Lily didn't know how to answer. She hadn't made any plans beyond the immediate. She had come back to put the past to rest, but seeing him again stirred feelings she hadn't expected.

"I'm not sure yet," she said quietly. "I guess I'm just figuring things out."

Ethan nodded, his smile fading slightly as he studied her. "I've been doing the same, in my own way."

Lily glanced at him, surprised. The boy she had once known as carefree and impulsive had grown into a man with a depth she hadn't anticipated. And yet, she couldn't help but feel the weight of their shared history between them.

There was so much left unsaid, so many emotions and memories that had never been addressed. The love, the betrayal, the heartbreak.

But perhaps, Lily thought, this was where it all began. This was the moment she had to face the past and decide what to do with it.

Chapter 2: The Weight of Silence

The minutes stretched on between them, heavy with unspoken words. Lily shifted in her seat, her hands trembling slightly as she wrapped them around the warm cup of coffee Ethan had ordered for her without asking. She had always loved how he remembered the little things, even after all these years. It was both a comfort and a curse.

Ethan leaned back in his chair, his gaze never leaving hers. The once carefree smile that had always been a part of him now seemed distant, as though something had changed beneath the surface. His eyes were filled with questions, but he didn't ask them. He didn't have to. Lily could feel the weight of everything they hadn't said, everything they had buried deep down, hanging between them like a silent storm.

"It's strange being back," Lily said, breaking the silence. Her voice felt foreign, like it didn't belong to her. "I didn't expect to come back like this, you know? After everything."

Ethan's expression softened, and he nodded, his lips pressing into a thin line. "I can imagine," he murmured. "I never thought I'd see you again, not after... well, not after the way things ended."

Lily closed her eyes for a moment, the memories rushing back with a painful clarity. The love, the promises, the way everything had fallen apart so suddenly. There had been so much left unsaid between them, so much left unresolved. But even then, she had never expected him to be the one who would hurt her the most.

"You don't have to apologize, Ethan," she said quietly, meeting his gaze once more. "I know what happened. I don't need explanations."

Ethan's eyes widened slightly, as if he had been expecting her to be angry, to lash out. Instead, Lily felt something different—something far more complicated. She didn't want to hate him. She didn't want to carry the bitterness she had held for so long. But forgiveness wasn't something she could just give away, not yet. Not when the wounds still stung.

"You don't have to forgive me," Ethan said softly, his voice rough around the edges. "I don't expect that. I just… I don't want to leave things like this. Not again."

Lily's heart fluttered at his words, and for a moment, the world outside the café seemed to fade away. It was just the two of them, caught in a space where time had stopped, where everything they had shared was still alive, hovering just out of reach.

"I don't know what to say," she admitted, her voice barely above a whisper. "I've spent so many years trying to forget, Ethan. Trying to move on. And now, here you are, and it feels like I'm still trapped in the past."

Ethan reached across the table, his hand hovering just above hers, but he didn't touch her. He didn't need to. The air between them was thick with something neither of them wanted to name. He understood. "Maybe it's not about forgetting," he said, his voice low. "Maybe it's about learning how to live with it. With what happened. And with who we've become since then."

Lily looked at him, really looked at him, for the first time in years. The boy she had once known seemed so far away now, but the man before her still held something—something familiar and comforting. It made her wonder, just for a moment, if they could ever find their way back to what they once had.

But the question was too painful to ask, too raw to even consider.

"I don't know what we're doing here, Ethan," she whispered, the uncertainty creeping into her voice. "I don't know if we can just pick up where we left off. But maybe... maybe we don't need to."

Ethan didn't respond immediately. Instead, he sat there, studying her with a quiet intensity, as if trying to read every emotion in her eyes. For a moment, it felt like they were back at the beginning, before everything had fallen apart. Before the silence. Before the hurt.

And just like that, Lily wasn't sure if she was ready to let go of what they had—or if she ever would.

Chapter 3: The Echo of the Past

The days that followed fell like a blur to Lily. She tried to convince herself that seeing Ethan again didn't change anything, but each passing moment only deepened the pull she felt toward him. The quiet, unspoken bond between them lingered, woven into the fabric of her everyday life. She couldn't escape it, not when every street corner, every café, every familiar place seemed to hold a memory of them—of the love they had shared and the pain that had followed. Yet, despite the constant reminder of their past, she tried to focus on the present. She had come back to Delford for closure, for peace. But it seemed the city was determined to remind her of the one thing she hadn't been able to move on from—Ethan.

One evening, a week after their encounter at the café, Lily found herself walking past his apartment building on Elm Street. It was an impulse, a decision she hadn't fully thought through. She wasn't sure what she expected to find, maybe a sign of him, or perhaps an answer to the question that had been haunting her since they had met again. She stood there for a few moments, her breath visible in the cool air, before she turned and walked toward the entrance. Her steps were hesitant, her heart pounding in her chest as the weight of the moment settled over her. She reached the door and paused, her hand hovering above the doorknob, unsure whether to knock or walk away. Before she could decide, the door opened. Ethan stood there, his expression surprised but not entirely unwelcome. "Lily," he said, his voice quiet, almost as if he had been waiting for her. "What are you doing here?" She swallowed hard, looking up at him, her pulse racing. "I... I don't know," she admitted. "I guess I just needed to talk. I needed to understand why everything feels so complicated." Ethan nodded, stepping aside to let her in. As she crossed the threshold into his apartment, she realized how much had changed in the years they had been apart—yet, in a way, nothing had changed at all. The same scent of coffee lingered in the air, the same soft light cast over the room. It was as though time had frozen in this space, just as it had between them. "Sit down," Ethan said softly, motioning toward the couch. Lily obeyed, feeling the weight of the years that had passed settle between them. They sat in silence for a while, neither knowing exactly where to begin. Finally, Lily spoke. "I don't know why I came here, Ethan. Maybe I'm looking for something I'm not even sure I deserve." He looked at her then, his eyes searching hers, as though trying to see into her soul. "You don't have to deserve anything, Lily. I'm not going to pretend I understand everything, but I know this much—what happened between us, it wasn't easy for either of us." She exhaled a long breath, her heart heavy with the weight of his words. She didn't know what to say in return, but for the first time in a long while, she felt like they might be able to find some sort of peace with each other, even if it was just in this moment. "I just want to know if it's possible," she whispered. "If it's possible to go back, to fix what we broke." Ethan was quiet for a long moment before he spoke. "I don't know," he said softly. "But maybe it's not about going back. Maybe it's about moving forward, together, without forgetting the past but learning how to live with it." Lily felt her chest tighten at his words. It wasn't the answer she had hoped for, but it was the one she needed. Slowly, she nodded, a small but significant step toward whatever future they could create. "Maybe you're right," she said quietly, looking up at him, her heart feeling a little lighter than it had before. "Maybe it's time to stop trying to fix the past and start figuring out what comes next."

Chapter 4: New Beginnings

The next few days passed in a haze. Lily found herself caught between the past and the present, walking through her days as if in a dream. She kept thinking about the conversation she had with Ethan, the one that had left so many things unspoken but still felt like a step toward something new. It was strange, this feeling of uncertainty mixed with hope, as if she were standing on the edge of something she couldn't quite see. But it felt different from the pain of the past. It wasn't the same. It was something else—something that hadn't been there before. Maybe it was a possibility.

On a sunny afternoon, Lily decided to take a walk to clear her mind. She had found a small park near the edge of the city, a quiet spot surrounded by trees, where the bustle of everyday life seemed to disappear. She had been here a few times before, always seeking solace in its stillness. Today, though, it felt different. She sat on a bench beneath a large oak tree, the warm sunlight filtering through the leaves, casting soft shadows on the ground. As she looked around, she couldn't help but smile at the peacefulness of it all. Maybe this was what she needed—space. Time to think, time to breathe, time to let go.

Her phone buzzed in her pocket, interrupting her thoughts. She pulled it out, expecting another work email, but instead, it was a message from Ethan. "Are you free tonight? I was thinking we could grab dinner and catch up more. No pressure, just... dinner." The simplicity of his words made her heart flutter, and she stared at the message for a long time before typing a reply. "Sure, I'd like that." She hit send before she could second-guess herself. For the first time in a while, she felt like she was opening herself up to something again—something she hadn't felt in years.

As evening approached, Lily found herself standing outside the small, cozy restaurant where they had agreed to meet. It was a place they used to come to during their college days, a quaint little Italian bistro tucked away in a quiet corner of the city. The familiar scent of fresh pasta and garlic filled the air, and for a moment, she could almost see them sitting at their usual table, laughing, talking about their dreams for the future. She shook her head, trying to push the memories away. This was a new chapter, she reminded herself. A new beginning. She wasn't the same person she had been back then, and neither was he.

She walked inside and saw Ethan waiting by the door, a casual smile on his face, but his eyes—those eyes—told a different story. They were filled with something Lily couldn't quite place. Was it anticipation? Nervousness? Or maybe it was just the weight of everything they had both been carrying for so long. "Lily," he greeted, his voice warm but with a hint of uncertainty. "Hey. I'm glad you could make it."

"Of course," she replied, smiling back at him, though her heart was racing. "It's good to see you."

They sat at the table, and for a while, neither of them spoke. The silence wasn't uncomfortable, though. It was a kind of unspoken understanding, a shared space where they could just be themselves without the pressure of trying to fix everything all at once. The waiter came by, taking their orders, and for a few moments, the world outside seemed to fade away.

"So," Ethan said after a while, breaking the silence, "how have you been? Really been, I mean."

Lily glanced at him, her heart skipping a beat. She could feel the sincerity in his question, and for some reason, it made her feel vulnerable, exposed. "I've been good," she replied, her voice steady despite the fluttering in her chest. "I'm just... trying to figure things out. It's been a strange few months. But I'm getting there."

Ethan nodded, his eyes never leaving hers. "I get that," he said softly. "I'm still trying to figure things out, too. I think we both are."

Lily smiled at that. There was something comforting in knowing that they weren't the only ones who felt lost, that they could both admit to the uncertainty that had been hanging over them. For the first time since they had met again, Lily felt like they were on the same page, moving toward something, even if it was still unclear what that something was.

They continued talking through dinner, the conversation flowing easily between them. They discussed their lives, their work, their friends, the things they had done since they had last been together. It was natural, almost as if they had never been apart. But with each passing moment, Lily found herself slowly letting go of the walls she had built around her heart. She was beginning to realize that maybe there was a chance for them, after all. Not to go back to what they once had, but to start something new. Something different. Something that wasn't weighed down by the past.

As the evening wore on, and the final course was cleared away, Ethan looked at her, his gaze soft and thoughtful. "Lily," he said, his voice low, "I know we've both been through a lot, and I don't want to rush anything. But I need you to know... I'm here. If you want to take things slow, or if you just want to talk, I'm not going anywhere."

Lily's heart melted at his words, and she felt a warmth spread through her chest. She had never imagined this moment would come, but now that it had, she couldn't help but feel a flicker of hope. Maybe it wasn't too late for them. Maybe they could find their way back, piece by piece, and build something new from the broken fragments of their past.

For the first time in years, she allowed herself to believe in the possibility of love once again.

Chapter 5: Uncharted Waters

The days after their dinner were filled with a quiet kind of anticipation. Lily couldn't quite pinpoint it, but something had shifted between her and Ethan. It wasn't an explosive change, but rather a subtle shift—a new energy that hummed just beneath the surface. It was as if they were both treading carefully, as though afraid of disturbing something fragile. But in that quiet space, there was also a sense of hope, a hope that maybe they were building something new, something worth pursuing.

Lily spent more time at the café where she had seen Ethan that first day. The familiar hum of the barista machines, the chatter of customers, the soft jazz playing in the background—everything felt comforting, as if the café had become her sanctuary. It was her place of peace, where she could reflect and gather her thoughts. She started writing again, something she hadn't done in months. It was almost as if her words were a way to process the whirlwind of emotions inside her—confusion, excitement, fear. There was so much she hadn't said aloud, but the pages of her journal were filling up with it all.

One afternoon, as she sat by the window, sipping her coffee and watching the world pass by, she felt the familiar buzz of her phone. Ethan's name appeared on the screen. "Would you like to meet up later? There's something I want to show you."

She stared at the message for a moment, unsure of what to expect. They had been taking things slow, but the invitation felt different this time. It felt personal, like he was inviting her into a part of his life that she hadn't yet seen. With a deep breath, she replied, "Sure, where?"

He responded quickly, "Meet me at the park in an hour. I'll explain when you get here."

Lily couldn't help but smile at the mystery in his words. She had no idea what he wanted to show her, but something told her it was important. She finished her coffee and made her way to the park, her heart beating a little faster with every step. The park was quiet, the trees swaying gently in the breeze, their leaves rustling softly. She spotted Ethan standing by a large oak tree, his back to her as he gazed out over the pond.

"Hey," she said, walking up to him.

Ethan turned around, his face lighting up when he saw her. "Hey," he said, his voice soft. "Thanks for coming. I know this is kind of random, but I wanted to show you something."

He led her down a path she hadn't noticed before, one that wound through a thick cluster of trees. The air felt different here, cool and crisp, as though they had stepped into a different world entirely. After a few minutes of walking, they arrived at a small clearing, where a wooden bench overlooked a hidden garden. It was tucked away, almost secret, surrounded by wildflowers and ivy. A small fountain trickled softly nearby, and the scent of blooming roses filled the air.

Lily stood there for a moment, in awe of the place. It was beautiful, untouched. "I had no idea this was here," she whispered.

Ethan smiled, sitting down on the bench and patting the space beside him. "I didn't either, not until a few weeks ago. I've been coming here whenever I needed to think. It's peaceful."

Lily sat next to him, her gaze lingering on the flowers. There was something almost magical about this place, like it was untouched by the chaos of the outside world. It felt like a secret, a secret he had shared with her.

"I wanted to bring you here," Ethan said, his voice quieter now, "because I think it's a place where we can talk about... well, about everything."

Lily turned to him, her heart skipping a beat. "Everything?" she asked softly.

"Yeah," he said, his eyes meeting hers. "I know we've both been avoiding the bigger questions, but maybe it's time to face them. About us, about what we want moving forward."

Lily nodded, feeling the weight of his words. This wasn't just a casual conversation—it was an invitation to confront what had been hanging between them for so long. They had both danced around their feelings, trying to avoid the uncomfortable truths that lingered in the space between them. But now, here they were, in a hidden garden, surrounded by the silence of the world, ready to face it all.

"I don't know what's going to happen, Ethan," Lily said, her voice trembling slightly. "I'm scared. Scared that if we try again, it might end the same way. But I also don't want to let go of what we could have."

Ethan's gaze softened, and he reached out, gently taking her hand in his. "I'm scared too," he admitted, his voice steady. "But I think we have a chance to get it right this time. We don't have to rush anything. We can take it one step at a time, see where it leads."

Lily squeezed his hand, feeling the warmth of his touch. For the first time, she didn't feel the need to rush, to push forward without understanding what they were building. She was willing to take things slow, to let their connection unfold in its own time. Maybe they could have the kind of love they had both dreamed of, one that wasn't overshadowed by the past. One that grew from the ground up, from trust, understanding, and patience.

As they sat there, side by side in the quiet garden, Lily realized that for the first time in a long while, she felt something she hadn't felt before—a glimmer of hope. It was uncertain, fragile, but it was there. And maybe that was enough for now.

Chapter 6: The Power of Patience

The weeks that followed were filled with small, quiet moments that felt more meaningful than anything grand. Ethan and Lily continued to meet regularly, their connection growing stronger each time. There was no rush to define their relationship, no pressure to move forward too quickly. It was as if they were both allowing each other the space to rediscover who they were, both as individuals and as something more, together.

They spent evenings in cozy cafés, mornings in the park, and long afternoons walking through the streets of the city. Each day felt like a new discovery, not just of each other, but of themselves. Lily found herself opening up more than she ever had before, sharing her fears, her dreams, the things that made her laugh and cry. And Ethan—he listened. He listened in a way that made her feel heard and understood, like she wasn't just a chapter in his life, but a part of a bigger story.

One rainy evening, they decided to take a walk by the river. The sky was overcast, the clouds heavy with the promise of rain, but neither of them minded. The soft patter of raindrops on the ground added to the feeling of intimacy, as if the world around them had faded into the background. The river shimmered under the dim streetlights, its surface rippling gently, and the scent of wet earth filled the air.

As they walked side by side, neither speaking, Lily felt a sense of calm that she hadn't known in years. There was no urgency, no need to make decisions or set expectations. For the first time, she could just be present in the moment, walking with someone who understood the weight of silence. Ethan was there, and he was content to simply walk beside her.

Eventually, they stopped at a bench overlooking the river. Ethan sat first, then patted the space next to him, inviting Lily to sit down. She did, pulling her jacket tighter around her as the cool breeze ruffled her hair.

"Do you ever wonder if we're doing the right thing?" Lily asked suddenly, her voice soft but sincere.

Ethan looked at her, his expression thoughtful. "What do you mean?"

"I mean," she continued, "all these little moments we've shared, they feel... right, you know? But sometimes I wonder if we're rushing into something we're not ready for. What if we're just holding on to the past because it's familiar, and we're not really looking at what's in front of us?"

Ethan was quiet for a moment, his eyes focused on the river before him. "I've thought about that too," he admitted. "It's easy to let the past dictate how we feel now. But I don't want to do that anymore. I don't want to move forward based on what we were, but on what we can be. I think we both need time, time to grow individually and together."

Lily nodded, feeling a weight lift from her shoulders. The uncertainty that had clouded her thoughts for so long seemed to fade with his words. They didn't have to rush, didn't have to force anything. What mattered was the journey, not the destination.

"I agree," she said quietly, "and I think that's exactly what we've been doing—taking our time. It feels right. We're not pretending to have all the answers, and maybe that's the best way to move forward."

Ethan smiled, his gaze meeting hers, and for the first time in a long while, Lily felt truly seen. He didn't need to fill the silence with words or grand gestures. His presence alone was enough to reassure her that they were on the right path. Slowly, he reached for her hand, his fingers intertwining with hers, grounding her in that moment. The simple act of holding hands seemed to say everything they hadn't spoken aloud.

As the rain began to fall harder, they decided to head back to the warmth of a nearby café. But the walk had done something to both of them. It had deepened their connection, grounded them in something that felt real, not forced. They didn't need to rush toward anything; they were content with the pace they were setting, allowing their bond to form naturally, without pressure or expectation.

Later that evening, as they parted ways at the door of Lily's apartment, Ethan kissed her gently on the cheek, a soft promise that lingered in the air. "I'm glad we're doing this, Lily. Whatever this turns into, I'm glad it's with you."

Lily smiled, her heart swelling with emotions she had buried for so long. "Me too, Ethan. Me too."

As she watched him walk away, the warmth of his words wrapped around her, and for the first time in a long time, Lily believed that love could be patient, that it didn't have to be rushed or forced. Love, she realized, was something that could be nurtured, like a delicate plant, growing slowly, but steadily. And maybe, just maybe, this time, they had the chance to grow together.

Chapter 7: The Unspoken Truth

The days stretched out in front of Lily like a canvas, blank and waiting to be filled. She and Ethan had reached a point where words seemed unnecessary; the quiet moments between them were enough to communicate the things they both wanted to say. But there was still something unspoken between them, something that neither of them dared to bring up.

It wasn't that they didn't trust each other—it was more about the fear of confronting the inevitable. Their pasts, the experiences that had shaped them, still loomed over their present, casting long shadows on the possibility of a future. Lily had spent so many years building walls around her heart, protecting it from the risk of pain, that now, even the smallest crack in those walls felt like a threat. Ethan, too, was guarded in his own way. He wasn't ready to rush into something serious, not with the history he carried.

And yet, neither of them could deny the connection that had formed between them. It was undeniable. Their days together were filled with laughter, quiet conversations, and moments that felt effortless. But the weight of the past lingered, holding them back from fully embracing the future.

One evening, after spending hours in a cozy bookstore café, sipping hot chocolate and discussing books they loved, they found themselves sitting side by side, neither speaking. The silence was comfortable, but the tension was there. It was as though they both knew the conversation they were avoiding, the one they needed to have in order to move forward. But neither of them seemed ready.

Lily couldn't help but feel a wave of frustration rising inside her. She had been patient, patient enough to let things develop on their own terms, but the uncertainty was beginning to gnaw at her. She needed to know. She needed to hear the words, to understand what Ethan wanted, what they both wanted.

Breaking the silence, Lily finally spoke, her voice quiet but steady. "Ethan," she began, her heart pounding in her chest, "where do we go from here?"

Ethan turned to look at her, his eyes meeting hers with a mixture of surprise and something else—something unreadable. For a moment, he didn't answer. He seemed to be weighing his words carefully, as though choosing the right ones was the most important thing.

"I don't know," he admitted, his voice soft. "I don't know what will happen next. But I do know that I want to keep spending time with you. I want to see where this goes, but I'm not ready to make promises I'm not sure I can keep."

Lily's chest tightened at his words, but she appreciated his honesty. It wasn't the answer she had hoped for, but it was the truth. Ethan wasn't ready to dive into something serious, and she wasn't sure she was either. They had both been through enough to know that love couldn't be rushed, no matter how much they might want it to be.

"I get it," she said, her voice barely above a whisper. "I'm not asking for promises. I just... I just need to know that we're not wasting time. That we're not pretending this is something it's not."

Ethan nodded, his fingers brushing against hers. "We're not wasting time," he said quietly. "I promise you that. I think we're just taking it one step at a time, and maybe that's all we need right now."

Lily swallowed the lump in her throat, her fingers tightening around his. "One step at a time," she repeated softly. "I can do that."

And with that, the air between them seemed to settle, the tension easing just a little. It wasn't a solution, not exactly. But it was a start. They had spoken the words they needed to say, and in doing so, they had allowed themselves to let go of the unspoken weight they had both been carrying.

As they sat there, side by side, in the soft glow of the bookstore's lamps, Lily felt something shift inside her. It wasn't a grand revelation, but it was enough. They were moving forward, slowly, carefully, but they were moving forward together. And for now, that was all that mattered.

Chapter 8: A Moment of Truth

The following weeks passed by in a blur of quiet moments, long conversations, and fleeting doubts that faded as quickly as they arose. Lily and Ethan had found a rhythm, an understanding that existed between them without the need for grand declarations. But as the days turned into weeks, Lily found herself wondering if they were truly on the same page or if they were simply avoiding the inevitable conversation.

Lily was the kind of person who felt things deeply, who internalized her emotions until they built up and exploded. She knew she couldn't keep avoiding the truth, especially when it came to Ethan. Her feelings for him had deepened, more than she had anticipated. What had started as a slow, steady connection had become something more—something undeniable. She couldn't ignore it anymore, nor could she keep pretending that things were fine just the way they were.

One chilly evening, after a walk through the park where they had exchanged nothing but lighthearted words, Lily found herself standing in front of Ethan's apartment building. She had arrived with every intention of talking, of finally addressing the feelings that had been growing inside her. But as she stood there, the weight of what she was about to say settled over her like a heavy fog.

Ethan had become more than just a companion to her. He had become someone she could imagine a future with. But was he on the same page? She wasn't sure.

Taking a deep breath, she entered the building and made her way up to his apartment. When the door swung open, Ethan greeted her with a warm smile, as though everything was exactly as it had always been.

"Hey, you," he said, stepping aside to let her in. "How was your day?"

"It was fine," Lily replied, her voice betraying the nervousness she felt. She followed him inside, her heart pounding in her chest.

They sat down on the couch, the comfortable silence between them now feeling heavy with unspoken words. Lily could feel the tension building inside her, a pressure she couldn't ignore. She had to say it. She couldn't hold back any longer.

"I've been thinking," she began, her voice shaky but determined. "I've been thinking about us, about where we're going, and what this is."

Ethan looked at her, his brow furrowed in curiosity. "What do you mean?"

Lily swallowed, her hands shaking slightly. "I mean... I need to know, Ethan. I need to know what this is between us. I can't keep pretending that I'm okay with just taking things one step at a time. I need more. I need to know if you see a future with me or if we're just going to keep doing this, unsure of what we're really doing."

Ethan's expression softened, and for a moment, he didn't speak. The silence between them stretched, each of them waiting for the other to break it. Lily's heart pounded in her chest, her thoughts racing. She had feared this moment for so long, but now that it was here, she realized it was the only way forward.

Finally, Ethan spoke, his voice calm but filled with emotion. "Lily, I... I can't give you all the answers right now. But I don't want to lose what we have. I care about you. I don't know exactly what the future looks like, but I want you in it. I want to see where this can go, even if it means taking our time and figuring things out as we go."

Lily felt a wave of relief wash over her, though she wasn't sure if it was the answer she had been hoping for. Ethan wasn't ready to commit fully, but he wasn't ready to walk away either. And for her, that was enough—for now.

"I can handle that," she said softly, her voice full of vulnerability. "I don't need you to have everything figured out. I just needed to hear that you're not going anywhere."

Ethan reached for her hand, his fingers warm against hers. "I'm not going anywhere," he said gently, his gaze locking with hers. "I promise."

For the first time in a long time, Lily felt the weight of her fears lift. The uncertainty still hung in the air, but it no longer felt like a burden. They didn't need to have all the answers. All they needed was each other, and the willingness to explore what lay ahead.

As the night wore on, they sat together, holding hands, the quiet comfort of their presence enough to fill the space between them. Neither of them knew exactly what the future held, but for the first time, Lily realized that the journey was just as important as the destination. And with Ethan by her side, she was ready to take the next step, whatever it might be.

Chapter 9: A Change of Heart

Days blurred into one another as the bond between Lily and Ethan grew stronger. The weight of uncertainty that had once lingered over their heads had begun to dissipate, replaced by a quiet confidence that perhaps they could navigate this complicated journey together. Still, there was an underlying tension—an unspoken understanding that, while things were moving forward, they weren't yet fully in sync. Ethan had made it clear that he wasn't ready to rush into anything too serious, but Lily couldn't help but wonder what he was truly thinking.

One crisp morning, Lily found herself at a café, waiting for Ethan. It had become their routine: Saturday mornings were for coffee and long conversations, the kind that left them both feeling like they had peeled back a layer of their souls. But today was different. Today, Lily had decided that she couldn't wait any longer. She needed answers. She couldn't continue walking this line of uncertainty, especially when her heart had already stepped across it.

When Ethan arrived, his smile was as warm as ever, but there was something distant in his eyes. Lily noticed it immediately—a subtle shift, something that told her that he wasn't entirely himself. They greeted each other, exchanged pleasantries, and sat down to their usual spot by the window.

The hum of the café around them seemed to fade away as Lily gathered her thoughts. She had prepared herself for this moment, but now that it was here, she felt a surge of nerves coursing through her.

"Ethan," she began, her voice steady but quiet. "We need to talk."

Ethan looked up, a flicker of concern crossing his face. "What's wrong?"

Lily took a deep breath, trying to steady her racing heart. "I've been thinking a lot about us," she said. "About where we're headed. And I just... I need to know if we're on the same page. I can't keep going around in circles, hoping for something that I'm not sure you want."

Ethan's expression softened, and for a moment, he looked away, his fingers tracing the rim of his coffee cup. "Lily..." he began slowly, as if choosing his words carefully. "I think about this too, more than I'd like to admit. But the truth is, I'm scared. I'm scared of rushing into something and messing it all up. I know what I feel for you, but I don't know if I'm ready to give you everything you deserve."

Lily's heart clenched at his words. She had known this was a possibility—had known that Ethan wasn't fully ready to give himself to her, at least not in the way she had hoped. But hearing it out loud hurt more than she expected.

"I don't need everything, Ethan," she whispered, her voice trembling with emotion. "I don't need perfection. I just need you to be with me. To stop holding back."

Ethan's gaze softened, and for the first time, Lily saw a flicker of vulnerability in his eyes. "I don't want to hurt you," he confessed, his voice low. "I don't want to lose you, but I'm not sure I'm the person you need me to be."

The pain in his words hit Lily harder than she cared to admit. She had spent so long convincing herself that they could work, that she could be patient and let things unfold naturally. But now, she realized something: no amount of patience could change the fact that Ethan wasn't ready to give her the certainty she craved. He wasn't ready to take that leap, and it was no one's fault—least of all his. It was just the way things were.

"I don't want to lose you either," Lily said, her voice thick with emotion. "But I can't keep waiting for something that may never come. I need more than what you're offering me."

For a long moment, neither of them spoke. The silence between them was heavy, laden with the weight of unspoken feelings. Finally, Ethan spoke again, his voice softer now, tinged with regret. "Maybe we're just not meant to be, not right now. I don't want to hurt you, Lily, but I can't give you what you need. Not yet."

Lily nodded, the tears threatening to spill over but never quite reaching the surface. "I understand," she said quietly, her heart aching. "I really do."

As they sat there, in the middle of the bustling café, it felt as if the world had shifted beneath them. It wasn't the answer Lily had hoped for, but it was the truth. And sometimes, the truth was the hardest thing to face.

Ethan reached across the table, taking her hand in his for the briefest of moments before pulling away. "I'll always care about you, Lily. You've changed my life in ways I didn't expect. But I don't know if I can be the man you need."

Lily didn't respond right away. She wanted to say something—anything—that would fix this, that would make everything go back to the way it was before the conversation had started. But she knew that wasn't possible. Sometimes, love wasn't enough to bridge the gap between two people who were simply not on the same path.

"I'll never forget you, Ethan," she said softly, her voice barely above a whisper. "But I think it's time we let go."

And with that, she stood up from the table, her heart heavy with the weight of their final goodbye. She walked out of the café without looking back, knowing that it was the only way to move forward—by leaving the past behind.

Chapter 10: A New Beginning

The days that followed were harder than Lily had anticipated. Despite knowing that letting go was the right decision, the ache in her chest didn't disappear as easily as she had hoped. She spent long hours lost in thought, trying to make sense of everything. Her heart had once been full of hope, brimming with dreams of a future she thought she could share with Ethan. But now, all she had were memories and a sense of emptiness that felt impossible to fill.

Lily threw herself into her work, hoping that staying busy would help her forget. She buried herself in projects, in late-night brainstorming sessions, and in the routine of her daily life. But no matter how much she tried, she couldn't escape the quiet spaces in her mind that always seemed to echo with thoughts of Ethan.

It was on one of these long evenings, while she was sitting at her desk with a cup of tea, that she heard the knock on her door.

"Lily?" a familiar voice called from the hallway.

It was her best friend, Maya.

Lily quickly wiped away the tear that had escaped and stood up, trying to hide the sadness that still lingered within her. Maya had been there for her through everything, and she knew she wouldn't let Lily shut herself off from the world.

"I'm here," Lily said, opening the door to see Maya standing there with a bright smile and a bag of takeout food in her hands.

"I come bearing comfort food and bad movies," Maya said, pushing past Lily into the apartment. "You're not getting out of this, by the way. You need to talk, and I'm not leaving until you do."

Lily let out a small laugh, grateful for Maya's presence. She had always been the one who could get through to her, the one person who could cut through the heaviness and remind her that life was still worth it , even after heartache.

They settled on the couch with their food, the two of them eating in silence for a moment before Maya finally spoke up.

"So, how are you really doing?" she asked, her tone soft but knowing.

Lily hesitated, glancing at her friend. "I don't know. Some days are okay, but others..." She trailed off, her voice thick with emotion. "It's hard to move on, Maya. I thought I was ready, but the emptiness is... overwhelming sometimes."

Maya nodded in understanding, setting down her food and turning to face Lily more fully. "I get it. You loved him. And now you're grieving. But you also have to remember that it's okay to take your time. You're not expected to bounce back overnight. Healing doesn't work that way."

Lily sighed, rubbing her eyes. "I know, but it feels like everything I thought I wanted is slipping away. I keep thinking about what could've been, about all the things I thought we could share together. And now... now it's just gone."

Maya reached out, placing a hand on Lily's shoulder. "It's hard to let go of someone you thought you were going to build a future with. But sometimes, the future we want isn't the one that's meant for us. Maybe Ethan wasn't the one for you, at least not in the way you thought."

Lily's heart tightened at Maya's words, but there was a flicker of truth in them. She had spent so much time holding on to the idea of what she and Ethan could be that she hadn't allowed herself to see the bigger picture. There were other futures out there—ones that she hadn't even imagined yet. And maybe, just maybe, she was ready to start creating a new one for herself.

"Do you think I'm being foolish?" Lily asked softly, looking at her friend for reassurance.

Maya shook her head. "No, Lily. You're not foolish for feeling heartbroken. You're not foolish for wanting something real and meaningful. But you're also not foolish for wanting to move forward. It's time for you to take a step for yourself, not for anyone else. You've got so much life left to live, and I know you'll find something that makes you happy."

The words settled in Lily's heart, stirring something inside her that had been dormant for far too long. It was time for a change, time to stop looking back and start looking ahead. It wouldn't be easy, but Lily knew it was the only way forward.

She smiled, her first genuine smile in days, and squeezed Maya's hand. "You're right. It's time for something new."

And so, for the first time in a long time, Lily allowed herself to think about the future—not about what was lost, but about what could still be. She didn't have all the answers yet, and she wasn't sure what the next chapter of her life would hold, but for the first time in weeks, she felt a glimmer of hope.

The journey ahead wouldn't be easy, but it was hers to take. And with that thought, Lily took a deep breath, ready to move forward and embrace whatever came next.

Chapter 11: Full Circle

Months passed, and the seasons shifted, bringing with them a subtle transformation in Lily's life. The crisp autumn air carried a sense of renewal, and for the first time in what felt like ages, Lily felt lighter. She had spent these months rediscovering herself, piecing her heart back together, and finding joy in the small, beautiful things that life offered.

Her mornings were filled with peaceful walks through the park, where the golden leaves crunched beneath her feet. Afternoons were spent in cozy cafés, sipping on warm lattes while working on her dream project—a book that reflected her own journey of love, loss, and self-discovery. Writing became her solace, her way of processing the whirlwind of emotions that had shaped her.

One evening, as Lily stood in the park watching the fiery hues of the sunset, she felt a quiet contentment. She hadn't thought much about Ethan in weeks, and the realization startled her. It wasn't that she had forgotten him; she knew she never truly would. But the weight of her memories no longer felt like a burden. Instead, they had become a part of her, woven into the fabric of her story, shaping her in ways she hadn't anticipated.

It was at that moment she heard a voice call out her name.

"Lily?"

Turning around, she saw a man standing a few feet away. The golden light of the setting sun illuminated his features, and for a heartbeat, her breath caught. It was Ethan.

He looked different—older, perhaps, or maybe it was the quiet vulnerability in his expression. "I wasn't sure it was you," he said, stepping closer.

Lily felt a mix of emotions surge through her—surprise, nervousness, and an unspoken curiosity. "It's been a while," she said softly.

Ethan nodded, his gaze meeting hers. "It has. How have you been?"

She hesitated, then smiled. "I've been... better. Finding my way again."

His eyes softened. "I'm glad to hear that. You deserve to be happy."

"And you?" she asked. "How are you?"

Ethan chuckled lightly. "I'm working on it. Life has a way of teaching you lessons when you least expect them." He paused, taking a breath before continuing. "I've thought about you a lot, Lily. About us. And I wanted to say... I'm sorry. For everything."

The sincerity in his voice caught her off guard, but instead of reopening old wounds, it brought a sense of closure she hadn't realized she needed.

"Thank you," she said, her voice steady. "I've thought about us too, and I've come to realize that some things aren't meant to last forever. But that doesn't mean they weren't meaningful."

Ethan nodded, a small, bittersweet smile tugging at his lips. "You've always had a way with words."

They stood there in silence for a moment, the past hanging between them like a delicate thread. Finally, Ethan extended his hand. "Friends?"

Lily looked at his hand, then back at him, and nodded. "Friends."

As they shook hands, Lily felt a sense of peace wash over her. She had come full circle, and for the first time, she truly felt free.

As Ethan walked away, disappearing into the distance, Lily turned back to the sunset. Life was unpredictable, she realized, but that was what made it beautiful. It was full of beginnings and endings, of chances lost and found, and of opportunities to grow.

With a renewed sense of purpose, Lily walked away from the park, her heart lighter than it had been in years. She didn't know what the future held, but she was ready to face it—on her own terms, with hope as her guide.

Because sometimes, the greatest love story you can have is the one you write

Thankyou for reading our novel till the end
We hope you liked this novel written
BY
<u>N.S. NANDVANSHI</u>

THANKYOU

Don't miss out!

Visit the website below and you can sign up to receive emails whenever N.S. Nandvanshi publishes a new book. There's no charge and no obligation.

https://books2read.com/r/B-A-XEDCD-XHDMF

Did you love *Romance Once Again*? Then you should read *Heartstrings*[1] by N.S. Nandvanshi!

Heartstrings – *A Love That Found Its Way Back*

When fate brings Aarav and Kavya back into each other's lives after years of silence, old emotions resurface, and unspoken words demand to be heard. As they navigate love, regrets, and second chances, they must decide—will they hold on to the past or embrace the love that never truly faded?

A heartfelt tale of lost love, rekindled hope, and a romance that was always meant to be.

---

1. https://books2read.com/u/3RG5RD

2. https://books2read.com/u/3RG5RD

Also by N.S. Nandvanshi

Romance Once Again
The Light Of Fates
Silent Desires
Forever Untold Affair
Velvet Scars
Heartstrings

About the Author

I am a professional writer and loves to write great books for the readers all over the world.

About the Publisher

www.ingramcontent.com/pod-product-compliance
Lightning Source LLC
Chambersburg PA
CBHW071510130726
47997CB00006B/2479